Brady Brady
and the B Team

Written by Mary Shaw
Illustrated by Chuck Temple

Scholastic Canada Ltd.
Toronto   New York   London   Auckland   Sydney
Mexico City   New Delhi   Hong Kong   Buenos Aires

Scholastic Canada Ltd.
604 King Street West, Toronto, Ontario M5V 1E1, Canada

Scholastic Inc.
557 Broadway, New York, NY 10012, USA

Scholastic Australia Pty Limited
PO Box 579, Gosford, NSW 2250, Australia

Scholastic New Zealand Limited
Private Bag 94407, Botany, Manukau 2163, New Zealand

Scholastic Children's Books
Euston House, 24 Eversholt Street, London NW1 1DB, UK

www.scholastic.ca

Library and Archives Canada Cataloguing in Publication

Title: Brady Brady and the B team / written by Mary Shaw ; illustrated by Chuck Temple.
Names: Shaw, Mary, 1965- author. | Temple, Chuck, 1962- illustrator.
Description: Series statement: Brady Brady
Identifiers: Canadiana 20189066571 | ISBN 9781443175319 (softcover)
Classification: LCC PS8587.H3473 B73195 2019 | DDC jC813/.6—dc23

Originally published in 2004 by Brady Brady Inc.
This edition published in 2019 by Scholastic Canada Ltd.

6 5 4 3 2 1   Printed in Malaysia   108   19 20 21 22 23

For Tom and Brad

It was the start of a new hockey season and Brady was excited.
He just knew this would be the best season ever for the Icehogs.

As always, Brady arrived first at the rink, followed by Tes.

The dressing room buzzed with chatter. Everyone was eager to get out on the ice. They would have to work hard, since their first game was tomorrow.

At the start of practice, Coach reviewed the drills on a chalkboard.

"Okay," he called out. "I want you all to loop around the pylons as fast as you can. Then *zip* over here and *zip* over there. Then pass the puck to another player who will take a shot on Chester. Wait a minute! Where is Chester?"

The dressing room fell silent. How were they going to do their drills without a goalie?

"I guess we'll have to cancel our practice," Coach said, shaking his head.

"Wait! One of us could go in net," Brady suggested.

"Yeah!" Tes agreed. "I'll get the spare equipment."

Everyone breathed a sigh of relief. Practice wouldn't be cancelled after all.

Tree was first to volunteer. He played goalie in street hockey. This couldn't be very different — he thought. Tree thought wrong. The ice was **waaay** too slippery, and the equipment was **waaay** too small.

Caroline tried next, but her glasses kept fogging up. She couldn't see a thing.

Then Tes took a turn. She twirled and spun, but didn't block a single shot.

Kev went in, but he never stopped talking until Coach asked him to collect all the pucks inside the net.

The first practice of the year was a *disaster*.
Everyone was disappointed.

Brady and Tes were saying good-bye outside the rink when they spotted Chester, running across the parking lot.

"Sorry I'm late!" Chester yelled. He was out of breath and dropping equipment with every step.

"Late? Practice is over!" said Brady. "Where were you?"

Chester bent to pick up his goalie pads.
"Uh, I just . . . there was something I had to do."

"But it was an important practice," Brady replied.
"Our first game is tomorrow!"

"I'm sorry, Brady Brady. I wanted to be here, but I . . . slept in."

Chester was making up excuses, but Brady wasn't sure why.

The next morning the dressing room was quiet. Everyone was nervous about the first game of the year — especially after such a horrible practice.

Tree hummed as he adjusted his shoulder pads, Caroline brushed her hair over and over, Kev talked non-stop, and Chester was . . .

. . . MISSING!

"Who'd like to take a turn between the pipes?"
asked Coach, swinging the goalie stick in the air.

Nobody volunteered.

Their knees shook and their teeth chattered as the Icehogs stepped onto the ice. They were playing an annoying team called the Hounds — without a ***real*** goalie!

It didn't take the Hounds long to start teasing.

"Hey, Icehogs! Aren't you gonna say your team cheer?
Here's one for you!"

*"We've got the power,
We've got the might,
We're going to lose big
With no goalie in sight!"*

The Icehogs did lose big that day . . . *really* big.
It was a terrible way to start the season.

"We got creamed out there," Caroline groaned, "all because of Chester."

"How could he do that to us?" asked Kev. "He really let us down."

Brady didn't like losing, but he refused to believe his friend would hurt the team on purpose. "He must have had a good reason to miss the game," he said.

At school the next day, Kev saw Chester talking to his teacher during recess. He was about to say hello, when he heard Chester say something about joining the "**B team**" and trying to win a championship.

Kev was upset. *Chester? On another hockey team?* he wondered.
That must be why he wasn't at the game yesterday!

On his way home from school, Kev caught up with Brady and told him what he'd overheard. Brady was shocked to learn that Chester was playing for a different hockey team. What would the Icehogs do without him? This would definitely NOT be their best year yet.

Brady could hardly sleep that night. He decided to talk to
Chester, first thing in the morning.

Brady was eating breakfast when Hatrick brought in
the morning paper.

Chester's picture was on the front page! Chester was on another team. But it wasn't a hockey team, it was a *BEE* team — a *SPELLING BEE* team

Brady ran to the phone. "You're in a Spelling Bee? Why didn't you tell us?"

"I didn't think I'd have to. I figured I'd be eliminated before I had to miss any games."

Then Chester whispered, "Besides . . . I was afraid everyone would laugh."

"I think it's great!" said Brady. "We thought you had joined another **hockey** team."

"I'd never be disloyal to the Icehogs," Chester replied. "But what am I going to do? The final round of the Spelling Bee is tonight. I'm so nervous. I hope I can still make it to the game."

"Don't worry about that, Chester," Brady told him. "We'll manage somehow. Good luck with the Spelling Bee."

Brady could hardly wait. He had one more call to make.

That afternoon,
Coach phoned all
the Icehogs and
asked them to come
extra early before
the game.

They met outside the arena.

"I'm afraid we may have to play without Chester again tonight," he told them.

Everyone gasped. So it was true! Chester had abandoned the Icehogs!

Coach held up his hand. "Wait," he said. "Brady Brady, why don't you tell them what's going on?"

"Chester's still an Icehog. He's competing in the Spelling Bee finals and he needs our support."

The Icehogs ran to the school. The gym was packed with people. Some kids sat in chairs on the stage, but one chair was empty — *Chester's!*

He was hiding backstage. "W-w-what are you guys d-d-doing here?" Chester mumbled through chattering teeth.

"We came to cheer you on, Chester," Brady replied.

"But . . . I . . . what about the game?" asked Chester.

"We can beat the Dragoons anytime," Tes replied. "You're part of our team, and a team sticks together."

Before Chester went on stage they huddled together for their team cheer:

"We've got the power;
We've got the might,
Chester's a great goalie,
Who can spell words right!"

Chester was doing very well when the Icehogs had to leave for their game. Brady gave his friend a thumbs-up as they hurried away.

The dressing room was quiet as the team laced up their skates. The Icehogs wanted Chester to win, but they had secretly hoped he would make the game. Now they would have to play without him — again.

Just then, Coach walked in.
"Listen up," he announced.
"You should all know that Chester is . . .

HERE!"

The Icehogs cheered as Chester dashed through the door. He was holding a gigantic medal and a framed certificate!

"Wow! You won!" Brady yelled.

"Yup! But I couldn't have done it without my team," Chester replied with a big grin.

As the team took to the ice, Brady put his arm around his friend.

"I forgot to ask. What was your winning word?"

Chester grinned. "***Dependability,***" he said.

"Definition please?" said Brady.

"I-C-E-H-O-G-S!" he spelled. Chester was back and this really would be the best season ever.